W9-BHU-610

Meyer

YEARLING BOOKS/YOUNG YEARLINGS/YEARLING CLASSICS are designed especially to entertain and enlighten young people. Patricia Reilly Giff, consultant to this series, received her bachelor's degree from Marymount College and a master's degree in history from St. John's University. She holds a Professional Diploma in Reading and a Doctorate of Humane Letters from Hofstra University. She was a teacher and reading consultant for many years, and is the author of numerous books for young readers.

For a complete listing of all Yearling titles,
write to Dell Readers Service,
P.O. Box 1045, South Holland, IL 60473.

Nate the Great
and the
HALLOWEEN HUNT

by Marjorie Weinman Sharmat
illustrated by Marc Simont

A Young Yearling Book

Published by
Dell Publishing
a division of
Bantam Doubleday Dell Publishing Group, Inc.
666 Fifth Avenue
New York, New York 10103

If you purchased this book without a cover you should be aware that this book is stolen property. It was reported as "unsold and destroyed" to the publisher and neither the author nor the publisher has received any payment for this "stripped book."

Text copyright © 1989 by Marjorie Weinman Sharmat
Illustrations copyright © 1989 by Marc Simont

All rights reserved. No part of this book may be reproduced or transmitted in any form or by any means, electronic or mechanical, including photocopying, recording, or by any information storage and retrieval system, without the written permission of the Publisher, except where permitted by law. For information address Coward-McCann, New York, New York 10016.

The trademark Yearling® is registered in the U.S. Patent and Trademark Office.

The trademark Dell® is registered in the U.S. Patent and Trademark Office.

ISBN: 0-440-40341-3

Reprinted by arrangement with The Putnam & Grosset Group on behalf of Coward-McCann

Printed in the United States of America

October 1990

10 9 8 7 6

WES

For Fritz
who loved to greet
all the ghosts and goblins

My name is Nate the Great.

I am a detective.

Tonight I got into trouble.

Tonight I was locked in a haunted house

with my dog, Sludge.

I was in big trouble.

1

There were no pancakes there.

I was on a case.

A Halloween case.

It started about an hour ago.

My dog Sludge and I were

looking out our window.

We were waiting for witches and clowns

and Draculas and princesses

to ring our doorbell.

Suddenly I heard a scratch at the door.

A loud scratch.

I went to the door

and opened it.

Someone was standing there

in a long dress, a bonnet, and shawl.

It was Little Red Riding Hood's

grandmother,

carrying a Trick or Treat bag

in her big teeth.

His big teeth.

The grandmother was Annie's dog,

Fang.

I, Nate the Great, did not think
that Halloween was a scary holiday.
Until now.
"Where is Annie?" I asked him.
"Does she know you're out alone
on Halloween?"
I did not wait for an answer.
I dropped some treats into Fang's bag.

5

He wagged his tail and
went down the walk.
I closed the door behind him.
Sludge crawled out from under a chair.
I said to him,
"Be brave on Halloween.
We do not believe in
ghosts and goblins.
Or grandmothers with big teeth."
Sludge went back to the window.
The doorbell rang.
I opened the door.
Annie and Rosamond were outside.
They were both dressed as
Little Red Riding Hood.
And they were each carrying a basket

covered with a red cloth.

"Your grandmother was just here,"
I said to both of them.

"I know it," Annie said.

"This is Fang's first year
out alone on Halloween."

"I put some treats in his bag," I said.

"And now I'll give you some
for your baskets."

"My basket is already heavy
with treats," Rosamond said.

7

"I can't carry any more."

"Mine isn't full yet," Annie said.

She lifted the napkin from her basket,

and I dropped some treats inside.

"I am finished with Trick or Treating,"
Rosamond said.
"I came here to ask
for your help."
"What kind of help?"
"One of my cats, Little Hex,
is missing," Rosamond said.
"He hates Halloween.
Every year he tries to hide.
But this year I can't find him."
"Where are your other three cats?"
I asked.
"Perhaps Little Hex is with them."
"Oh no," Rosamond said.
"Every Halloween
Super Hex, Big Hex, and Plain Hex

9

go to the old haunted house
on the next street and help to haunt it.
But Little Hex is too scared,
so he hides."
"Wait until tomorrow," I said.
"Halloween will be over,
and Little Hex will come out
of his hiding place."
"But he might be really lost,"
Rosamond said.
"I'm so worried

10

I can't eat any of my treats.

Please help me."

"Very well. I, Nate the Great,

will take your case.

Tell me, when was the last time

you saw Little Hex?"

"He was following Annie and me,"

Rosamond said.

"Where did you go tonight?" I asked.

"First I put on my costume,"

Rosamond said, "and then I went to

Annie's house.

Little Hex followed me there."

"And then what?"

"Annie finished dressing up Fang.

She sent him on his way.

Then Annie and I went to

Claude's house. He gave us some

cookies.

We put them in our baskets.

Next we went to Esmeralda's house.

She gave us her special

Halloween biscuits."

"Was Little Hex still following you?"

"Yes," Rosamond said.

"Then Esmeralda asked Annie and me

to help her get into her gorilla costume.

So Annie and I stepped into her house.

And Little Hex did too.

Annie and I helped

Esmeralda become a gorilla.

13

The three of us started
to leave Esmeralda's house.
That's when I noticed
that Little Hex was gone."
"Then he's probably still
in Esmeralda's house," I said.
"No, we looked everywhere
in her house," Annie said.
"Was Esmeralda's door open or closed
while you were helping her
with her costume?" I asked.
"Open," Annie said.
"So Little Hex probably

escaped outside," I said.

"It is hard to find

a small black cat in the dark.

But I will go out

and hunt for him."

"Oh thank you," Rosamond said.

"I will go home and wait

for you to bring him back."

Rosamond and Annie left.

I wrote a note to my mother.

Dear mother,
I am on a Halloween case.
I am hunting for little Hex,
who would rather hide than hunt.
I will be back (unless a
grandmother with big teeth
uses them on me)
Love,
Nate the Great

I got a flashlight.

Sludge and I went out into the night.

I saw two pirates ahead of us.

"Excuse me," I said, "have you

seen Rosamond's cat, Little Hex?"

The pirates turned around.

They were Finley and Pip.

16

"We have just started
on our rounds," Finley said.
"And all we've seen
are a dancing artichoke
and a robot."

17

Sludge and I walked
up and down the street.
We saw more pirates.
And monsters and kings
and artichokes.
But we did not see Little Hex.
Where could he be?
"What would a scared cat do
on Halloween?" I asked Sludge.
Then I had an idea.
Perhaps Little Hex wasn't scared
anymore.
Perhaps I should be looking
for a brave cat
and not a scared one.
"Perhaps this year

Little Hex is learning how to haunt,"
I said to Sludge.
"I, Nate the Great,
don't believe in haunted houses.
But we must go to that old house
and hunt for Little Hex."
Sludge did not look happy.
But we walked to the old house.

It looked haunted.

It looked like every ghost

who had ever haunted anything

was haunting this house

on this night.

Sludge and I crept up the front steps.

They creaked.

I knew they would.

I knocked on the door.

It creaked.

I knew it would.

I opened the door.

It squeaked.

I knew it would.

I stepped into the house.

Sludge slunk in.

I called out,

"Super Hex, Big Hex, Plain Hex,

Little Hex, any Hex, are you here?

You have one minute to show your

faces. Then Sludge and I are leaving."

I started to count the seconds.

"One, two, three, four . . ."

SLAM!

The door shut behind us.

I tried to open it.

It was stuck.

"There must be another door,"

I said to Sludge.

I flashed my flashlight around.

I saw cobwebs, and old furniture

draped with white sheets.

I heard clinking and clanking

and shrieking.

"Is that you, cats?" I shouted.

I saw three pairs of eyes

glowing at me in the dark.

Cats' eyes.

They belonged to Super Hex, Big Hex

and Plain Hex.

Then they disappeared.

I flashed my flashlight

all over the house.

The three cats were gone.

But how did they get out of the house?

How could Sludge and I get out?

I heard more clinks and clanks

and shrieks.

The cats had left,

so what was making

those ghostly noises?

I, Nate the Great,

now believed in haunted houses.

We had to get out of here!

I found another door.

It was locked.

I tried windows.

They were locked.

"There must be a way out," I thought.

"The cats got in and got out."
I kept looking.
And then, in front of me
I saw a ghost!
I don't believe in ghosts,
so how could I see one?
But it was creeping toward me
dressed in a white sheet.
And suddenly I knew
I had solved the case.
Little Hex must be under that sheet,
learning how to haunt.

26

I lifted the sheet.

Sludge was huddled under it.

He was hiding.

I unwrapped him.

He led me to another room.

He found a hole.

It was small.

But he dug in it, making it bigger.

It was big enough for us to crawl into.

It led to the outside.

We were free.

"Good work, Sludge," I said.

We walked down the street,

away from the house.

We were happy to do that.

"Little Hex was not

in the haunted house," I said.

"We are back to looking

for a scared cat."

Did I have any clues?

Pancakes help me think.

Bones help Sludge think.

We went home.

We ate.

I thought back.

The last time Rosamond saw Little Hex

was when he followed her into

Esmeralda's house.

Then he was gone.

Esmeralda and Annie and Rosamond

had searched Esmeralda's house.

But they could not find Little Hex.

30

So he must have gone out

into the night.

Alone.

But why would he do that

when he was scared of Halloween?

Sludge was scared of Halloween, too.

He had hidden under a chair

in my house and under a sheet

in the haunted house.

Perhaps Little Hex was hiding

under something.

But where?

"We must go where Little Hex

was last seen," I said.

Sludge and I went

to Esmeralda's house.

31

She was there,

eating from her bag of treats.

"I am looking for Little Hex," I said.

"He isn't here," Esmeralda said.

"Rosamond and Annie and I looked

all over this house.

Want some of my treats?

My bag got too heavy to carry

around."

I stared at Esmeralda's treats.

Suddenly I remembered something.

I remembered lots of things.

I remembered *clues*.

"I have no time for treats," I said.

"I must go to Rosamond's house

right away."

Sludge and I rushed
to Rosamond's house.
She was lying on a sofa.
She was still wearing her
Little Red Riding Hood costume.
She looked strange in it.
Rosamond looked strange in everything.
"I was just at Esmeralda's house,"
I said. "She was eating
some of her treats."
"I'm still not hungry," Rosamond said,
pointing to her covered basket
on a table. "I'm too sad to eat."
"I think I know where Little Hex is,"
I said.
"Where? Where is he?"

34

Rosamond clutched her red cloak.

I, Nate the Great,

walked over to Rosamond's basket.

I lifted up the red cloth

that was on top of it.

And there was Little Hex,
fast asleep in the basket!
"It's Little Hex!" Rosamond cried.
"Yes," I said. "I, Nate the Great,
say that you've been carrying him

36

around ever since you left
Esmeralda's house."

"I *have?*"

"Yes. He must have crawled
into your basket at Esmeralda's house
while you and Annie were busy
helping Esmeralda become a gorilla."

"But how could he fit inside?"
Rosamond asked.

"Where are the treats I collected?"

"There are a few left in the basket,"
I said. "Little Hex probably ate
most of them
and took their place
under the napkin
and hid there.

Sludge hid under a chair

and a sheet tonight.

When you're scared,

you might hide under something.

Sludge gave me that clue twice."

Rosamond stroked Little Hex.

"But how did you know that

Little Hex was hiding

in my basket?" she asked.

"He could have been hiding anywhere."

"You gave me the clue," I said.

38

"You told me that you and Annie
started out together,
doing Trick or Treat.
When you got to my house,
Annie had room in her basket
for treats, but you said
your basket was too heavy.
How come your basket
was heavier than Annie's?
They should have been the same
because you both went to
the same places.
I, Nate the Great,
say that your basket
was full of Little Hex
and he was full of your treats.

39

No wonder it was heavy."

"I'm so happy to have

Little Hex back," Rosamond said.

"Let's have a Halloween party

to celebrate.

I'll go outside and invite

everybody I see."

"Including your grandmother

with the big teeth?" I asked.

"Sure," Rosamond said.

"Fang probably collected more treats

than anybody."

"I believe that," I said.

"But I will never be

hungry enough to take

food from Fang's fangs."

Sludge and I left.

The case was over.

Halloween was almost over.

No more hunting, no more haunting.

What had caused all the

clinking and clanking

and shrieking

in that old haunted house?

41

I would never know.

I, Nate the Great, say that
some mysteries are better left
unsolved.